High Flyer With a Flat Tire

High Flyer With a Flat Tire

Written by Paul McCusker

Illustrated by Karen Loccisano

PUBLISHING

Colorado Springs, Colorado

HIGH FLYER WITH A FLAT TIRE

Library of Congress Cataloging-in-Publication Data

McCusker, Paul, 1958-
High Flyer with a flat tire / Paul McCusker ; illustrations by Karen Loccisano.
p. cm. — (Adventures in Odyssey ; 2)
Summary: After having a fight with the local bully, Mark is falsely accused of vandalism and sets out with his friends to solve the crime.
ISBN 1-56179-100-8
[1. Vandalism—Fiction. 2. Bullies—Fiction. 3. Conduct of life—Fiction.]
I. Loccisano, Karen, ill. II. Title. III. Series: McCusker, Paul, 1958- Adventures in Odyssey ; 2
PZ7.M47841635Hi 1992
[Fic]—dc20
91-10
CIP
AC

Published by Focus on the Family Publishing, Colorado Springs, CO 80995.

Distributed in the U.S.A. and Canada by Word Books, Dallas, Texas.

Editors: Sheila Cragg and Janet Kobobel
Designer: Sherry Nicolai Russell
Cover and Interior Illustrations: Karen Loccisano

Adventures in Odyssey Radio Drama
(A Focus on the Family Production)
Creators: Phil Lollar, Steve Harris
Executive Producer: Chuck Bolte
Scriptwriters: Phil Lollar, Paul McCusker
Production Engineers: Dave Arnold, Bob Luttrell

Printed in the United States of America

92 93 94 95 96 / 10 9 8 7 6 5 4 3 2 1

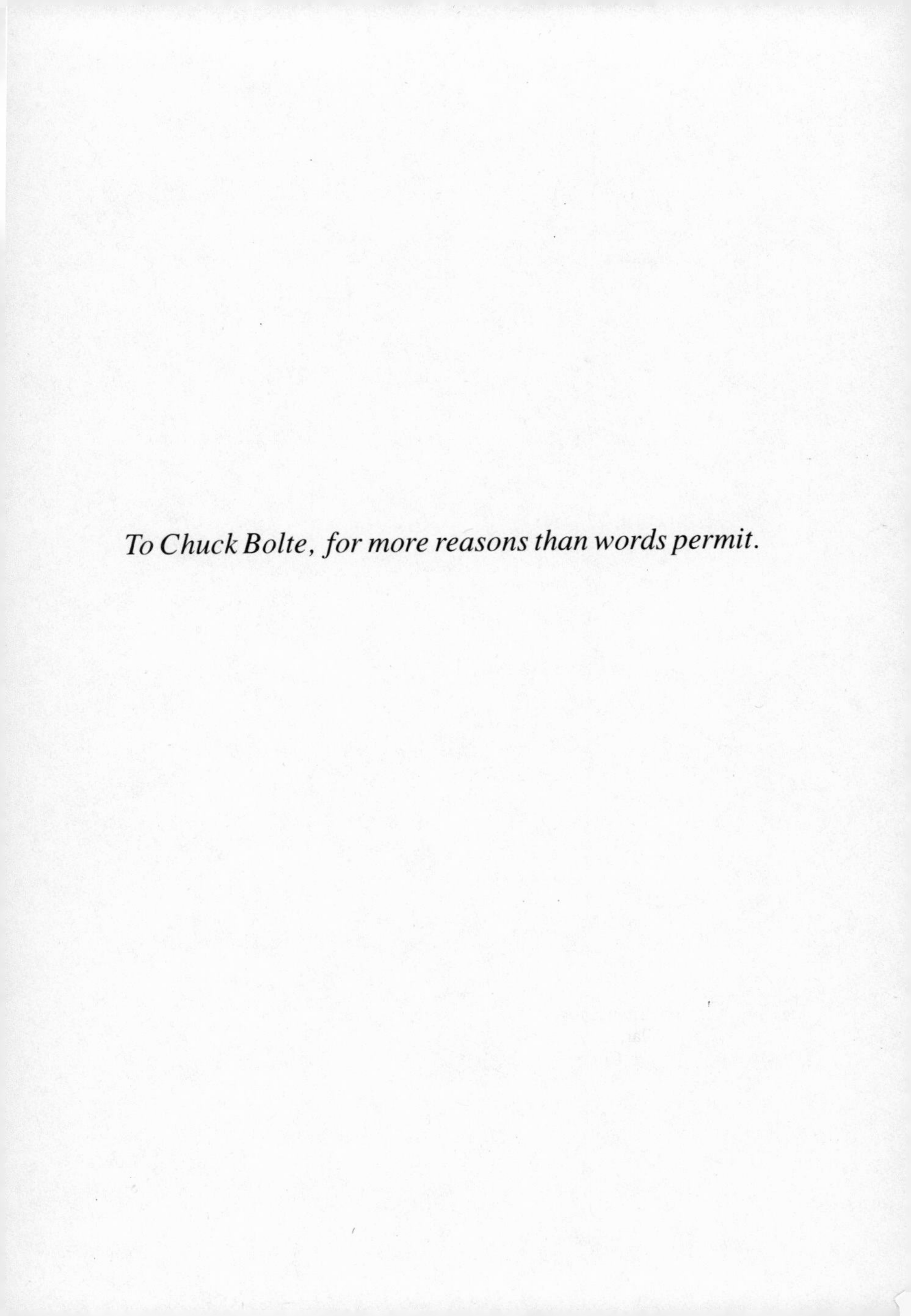

To Chuck Bolte, for more reasons than words permit.

Contents

CHAPTER ONE

The Trouble Begins

Mark! Hey, Mark."

Mark Prescott looked up expectantly. He had been watching a group of boys play basketball in McAlister Park. Like most Saturday mornings since arriving in Odyssey, he had waited an hour for someone to ask him to join the game. He thought the moment had arrived.

"Mark!" Patti Eldridge called across the green expanse of park.

Mark cringed. Patti and a girl he didn't know were riding their bikes toward him. A few weeks ago when he met Patti, she had decided she was going to be his best friend. Mark wasn't happy about the idea. He liked Patti well enough, but it was embarrassing for boys to have girls as friends—even if she did a lot of boy-type things. As if to prove the point, Patti let out a wild yell, pulled the front of her bike into the air and did a wheelie down the path.

"We're going to Whit's End. You want to go?" Patti asked breathlessly as she and her friend stopped alongside Mark. "Oh, uh, Mark," Patti said, "this is Rachel Morse. Rachel, this is Mark Prescott. He's the one I told you about."

"Nice to meet you," Rachel said, hardly above a whisper. She glanced away shyly.

Mark nodded. Rachel was a chubby girl with large blue eyes and freckles dotting her round cheeks.

"So, let's go!" Patti urged.

Mark looked back at the boys and their basketball game. "Okay," he said with a shrug.

Together, they started walking across the park. Patti stopped for a moment and pushed her loose sandy hair up under her baseball cap. Mark's eye caught sight of a tiny red dot near her temple.

Patti must have noticed Mark's glance because she suddenly turned her face away. "Don't look at it! It's like a volcano."

"What?" Mark asked innocently.

"You saw it. You know. It's a zit," Patti mumbled.

She turned to Rachel. "You said nobody would notice. I told you they would."

"A zit?" Mark wasn't sure what the fuss was about. "You mean a pimple?"

"Yes, what other kind is there?" she shouted.

"I . . . I don't know." Mark felt awkward. Patti had never yelled at him like this. "What's the big deal?"

"You're a boy," Patti added. "You wouldn't understand."

Mark had to agree; he didn't want to know about Patti's pimples.

"Oh no, look who's coming," Patti moaned. "Just what I don't need."

Like cowboys on wild horses, Joe Devlin and his gang rode toward them, stirring a cloud of dust as they weaved their bicycles across each others' paths.

"Let's just walk on," Mark whispered to Patti. "Maybe they'll ride past us."

"Ha!" said Patti.

Joe and his gang surrounded Mark, Patti and Rachel.

"Well, well, well, look who's out for a Saturday morning stroll," Joe said with a sneer.

"Yeah, look who it is!" Joe's younger brother Alan piped in.

"Shut up, Alan, or I'll make you go home," Joe snapped.

Alan hung his head and closed his mouth.

Joe turned to Patti. "Where are you headed, Patti? Is it playtime at Whit's End?"

"None of your business, Joe," Patti said. "Just leave us alone."

Joe stuck his bottom lip out in a mock pout, "Aw, can't we come play with you?"

"Whit's End is open to everybody. Go on if you want," Patti replied with an air of formality.

"But we want to go with you," Joe pleaded in a whiny voice, getting a laugh from his gang.

"Get out of our way!" Patti shouted, shoving past him. She caught Joe off guard and sent his bike crashing to the ground.

Mark took a sharp, deep breath and braced himself. Rachel watched wide-eyed.

Joe quickly picked up his bike and examined it. "You're in for it now, Patti. If you hurt my new bike, I'm going to do some major damage to you."

"New bike! Is that a new bike?" Mark asked brightly.

"Yeah. A ten-speed High Flyer!" Joe announced. "It can outrun any bike in town. And there better not be any scratches on it."

"Who cares?" Patti returned. She gestured for Mark and Rachel to follow. "Come on, guys."

Joe grabbed Patti's arm and said, "I didn't give you permission to leave."

Patti tried to pull her arm away, but Joe held firm.

"Ow!" Patti cried. "Let go."

Joe laughed. "I told you I didn't give you permission to

leave. Ask for it!"

Patti struggled to get free, but Joe twisted her arm to keep his hold. Mark was about to jump into the tug-of-war when a loud, commanding voice shouted, "Let go of her!"

Startled, everyone turned to the unlikely source of the outburst. Rachel put her hand over her mouth and blushed.

Joe gave Patti a shove as he let go of her arm.

Then he glared at Rachel in a mocking way and asked, "Did you say something to me, fatso? Did a voice really come out of that barrel of blubber?"

Mark stiffened. He could think of few things more insulting than picking on someone's weight problem. Rachel lowered her head.

"Be quiet, Joe. That's no way to talk," Mark said as he stepped between Joe and Rachel.

"Stay out of this, press-snot," Joe snorted. "El blubbo can get on her bike and ride off anytime she wants, if her bike can hold all that weight. You got special shock absorbers, Rachel?"

"Shut up, Joe!" Mark shouted.

"Don't listen to this ignoramus," Patti said to Rachel.

"I'd rather be an ignoramus than a fat-oramus," Joe snickered.

"You're a jerk, Joe!" Patti said, clenching her teeth.

Mark turned to Rachel and said, "Let's go."

It was too late. Rachel's face was turning red as she

strained to keep from crying. Then large tears formed in her eyes and rolled down her cheeks. When she climbed onto her bike, she started sobbing.

"Rachel," Patti said, stepping toward her, but Rachel pushed her bike forward and took off pedaling up the path.

"Rachel!" Patti called.

Right before Rachel disappeared around the bend, Mark spotted an unfamiliar blond-haired boy on his bike. He came from behind a tree and called Rachel's name, but she didn't stop. He darted an angry look in their direction and then rode after her.

"Can't take a joke," Joe chuckled.

"You creep!" Patti roared and threw a punch at Joe. He quickly stepped back but tripped over his brother's feet and fell. Patti moved toward him with her fists clenched.

"Patti! Stop!" Mark yelled, grabbing her arm.

Her eyes ablaze, she turned; for a moment, Mark thought she was going to take a swing at him, too.

Joe sat on the grass and shouted a stream of bad names at Patti. Alan extended a hand to help him up, but Joe slapped it away.

"Get lost!" he spat and got up by himself. "Just stay out of my way."

Patti shook a finger at Joe. "Don't you ever talk to Rachel like that again."

"Why don't you try something now when I'm ready for you? Come on, tomboy. Try to fight me now."

"Don't do it," Mark said.

"That's right," Joe jeered. "Listen to your boyfriend."

"Shut up!" Patti yelled.

"Don't pay attention to him," Mark said to Patti. "My dad says that sooner or later guys like him get what they deserve."

"Guys like who?" Joe jibed.

"Guys like you who go around and start trouble for no reason," Mark returned.

Joe smiled sarcastically. "What does your dad know about anything? He's not even around. Right? That's why you and your mom came to Odyssey. I've heard all about it. Your dad doesn't like you, so he left you."

Mark threw a wild punch that grazed the side of Joe's face.

"You're going to be sorry for that," Joe shouted, tackling Mark. They fell into the dirt, tossing up a cloud of dust as they rolled over each other, struggling to pin the other one underneath. Mark swung his arms furiously, his elbow connecting with Joe's mouth. This dazed Joe enough for Mark to climb on top.

"It's the police!" someone shouted. "Police! Let's get out of here!"

Mark looked up. Joe threw Mark off his chest and gave him a blow to his cheek.

"Joe, police!" Alan cried out, pulling at his brother.

Patti grabbed Mark. "Give it up, Mark!"

Breathless, dirty and sweaty, Mark and Joe strained against the arms that held them.

"You jerk! You better hope we're never alone to finish this fight," Joe yelled. His lower lip was split and bleeding.

Mark shouted back, "Anytime, Joe! You'll get what you deserve. You'll see."

Joe and his gang jumped on their bikes and rode off. Mark glanced around for the policeman who had scared everyone away. Across the park he saw Officer Hank Snow watching them. His arms were folded, and his expression was one of silent rebuke.

"He should arrest those guys," Patti said.

Mark tried to dust himself off and then shoved his shirt-tail back into his jeans without much care.

"Do you still want to go to Whit's End?" Patti asked as she picked up her bike.

"No," Mark answered. "I better go home."

He took one last look at Joe, wreaking confusion among Odyssey's Main Street traffic. He was cycling recklessly between the cars. Mark wished someone would get Joe and get him good.

"Ouch!"

Mark Prescott dropped the washcloth into the bathroom sink and then stretched upward to get a better look at his face in the mirror. The red lump next to his right eye seemed to be growing.

"Oh, great," he moaned to himself, noticing the small bruise on his left cheek. "Mom's going to kill me."

He picked up the damp washcloth again, dabbed it on the sore spots and groaned from the sharp, jabbing pain. Then he ran his fingers through his dark brown hair and checked himself in the mirror one last time.

"The red lump doesn't look too bad," he assured himself.

The scratch could easily be explained to his mother. It wouldn't be an outright lie to say he had fallen, would it? He considered telling her the whole story, but he was afraid it would upset her. She had enough on her mind without worrying about Mark getting into fights. And it would hurt her if she knew the kids were saying things about Mark's dad and their separation.

Mark decided he couldn't tell her the truth. They were still the new people in town, and his mother was nervous about making a good impression. Getting in a fight, no matter whose fault it was, rarely ever left people with good impressions. Besides, Mark didn't want to get punished.

He threw the washcloth into the hamper, went to his room and put on a clean shirt and a favorite pair of jeans.

Just like new, he thought as he walked down the stairs.

Jumping the bottom two steps, he could see his mother through the living room doorway. She was sitting on the love seat, her hands knotted in her lap. Her glance caught Mark's.

"Come in here, son," she called with a worried tone that Mark knew well.

As he stepped through the doorway into the living room, he saw why. A stern-looking woman was sitting on the couch, holding a slashed bicycle tire that looked like chopped black licorice.

Joe Devlin was sitting next to her.

CHAPTER TWO

Accused!

Mrs. Devlin's face was pinched into lines of disapproval. She waved her hand accusingly at Mark. "If you don't believe me, just take a look at your son's face. He was in a fight with my Joseph, Mrs. Prescott. One look at his face proves it."

Mark glanced at Joe. A large scrape went down the side of his face, and his lower lip was swollen. Mark felt a moment's satisfaction that Joe looked like he had gotten the worst of the fight.

"Mark, were you and Joe in a fight today?" Mrs. Prescott asked.

"Yeah, Mom, but—"

Mrs. Devlin interrupted. "No 'buts' about it, young

man. Simply answer the question."

"Yes, ma'am. We were in a fight today."

Mrs. Prescott frowned. "Who started it?" she asked.

"Mark did," Mrs. Devlin answered, as if she had seen the fight herself.

"What!" Mark shouted with disbelief.

"According to my Joseph," Mrs. Devlin said, glaring at Mark, "you picked a fight while he and his friends were riding their bikes through McAlister Park."

"My new bike," Joe added sadly.

"Your Joseph is lying!" Mark blurted out.

"Mark!" his mother warned.

"But it's true, Mom. Patti and Rachel and I were going to Whit's End and—"

"Yes, and that Patti. I don't know what to make of a girl who goes around beating up boys," Mrs. Devlin said.

"She didn't beat me up, Mom," Joe quickly corrected her. "She just tried to."

Mark anxiously rocked from one foot to the other. "Joe started it! He always starts it."

"Liar!" Joe screamed, leaning forward as if he were going to leap off the couch. Mrs. Devlin put a restraining hand on his arm.

"He picked on Patti and called Rachel names, and then he said—" Mark stopped himself. He didn't want to repeat what Joe had said about his father, not in front of his mother.

"What else did he say, Mark?" Mrs. Prescott asked.

"Nothing." Mark looked down at the floor. The room was weighted in silence for a moment.

Finally, Mrs. Prescott spoke. "Regardless of who started it, Mark, I think you should apologize to Joe for fighting with him. You know better than to behave like that."

"But, Mom—" Mark looked at her helplessly.

She was resolute. "Go on, son."

Mark mustered his strength to keep from saying what he really wanted to say. Then he muttered, "I'm sorry, Joe."

Joe looked at him with a smug expression of victory.

"And now," Mrs. Devlin began, "there is a financial matter to take care of."

Mark and his mother exchanged uneasy glances.

Mrs. Devlin held up the slashed tire. "I expect Mark to pay for a new tire for my son's bike."

Mark's mouth fell open.

Mrs. Prescott stammered, "Why, why should Mark pay for the tire?"

"Because he is obviously the one who cut it to pieces!" Mrs. Devlin announced grandly, like a detective who had just solved a murder case.

"I didn't do it! I don't know anything about his tire!" declared Mark.

Mrs. Devlin looked at Mark with strained patience.

"Please, young man, you'll only make things worse by lying more than you already have. Everyone at the park heard you say you would get back at my Joseph. Clearly you followed him to Whit's End after he beat you in the fight and slashed his tire while he was inside. It's an open-and-shut case of revenge."

"It's not true!" Mark exclaimed, turning to his mom. "I came home after the fight, ask Patti."

"Asking Patti won't do any good. Naturally she'll side with Mark. They're best friends," reasoned Mrs. Devlin.

"Boyfriend and girlfriend," Joe added.

"She was probably in on the whole thing," Mrs. Devlin concluded.

"No!" Mark protested. "I came straight home! You were here, Mom. You know."

Mrs. Prescott shook her head. Of course, Mark realized, she *didn't* know. He had sneaked in the house so she wouldn't see his marks from the fight. Mark slumped despondently.

"Well?" Mrs. Devlin prodded.

"I think we'll have to discuss it, Mrs. Devlin," Julie Prescott said, rising from the chair.

Mrs. Devlin took the hint and stood as well. "Discuss it? Discuss it as much as you like, just as long as we get our money for the tire. I would hate to involve the police."

Joe smirked at Mark.

"I'm sure we'll get this all worked out," Julie said.

Mrs. Devlin agreed that they most certainly would.

Mark's mom walked Mrs. Devlin and Joe to the front door while Mark waited in the living room. They left the slashed tire on the floor.

When his mother returned, she gestured for Mark to sit down on the couch. "Now, do you want to tell me what really happened?"

Mark told her everything, from watching the basketball game that morning through to his fight with Joe. He left out Joe's comments about his father, though. He made it sound like he got in the fight to protect Patti and Rachel, which was partly true.

Julie took Mark's face in her hands. "Why didn't you tell me about this as soon as you got home?"

Mark tried to look away, but his mom's grip was firm. "I didn't want you to get upset," he said.

She caressed his cheek, lightly touching the scratch and examining the red lump next to his eye. "Oh, Mark."

Mark felt sorry for causing so much trouble. He should have told his mom everything when he got home. Why hadn't he talked to her?

"What are we going to do about the tire?" his mother asked softly.

Mark wondered the same thing and shrugged. They could pay for it, but that would be the same as admitting guilt. Then Mark would have a reputation as a vandal. He didn't want that. But what could he do? How could he prove he didn't do it?

He thought about it and then suddenly smiled at his mother. Kicking at the tire next to his feet, he said, "I know, Mom! It'll be easy."

His mother looked at him skeptically.

His eyes were alight with the flame of a good idea. "All I have to do is find out who really *did* slash the tire!"

CHAPTER THREE

The Scene of the Crime

Mark was reaching for the front doorknob to Whit's End when someone called his name. He turned to see a couple of boys coming toward him on the sidewalk. He remembered them from somewhere, Whit's End probably, but he had no idea who they were.

"I heard how you whipped Joe," the first boy said.

"Yeah?" Mark said vaguely. He didn't want another fight if these were two of Joe's friends.

"Yeah," the second boy said. "Good job. Joe's been needing it for a long time."

"Yeah, cool," the first boy said.

Mark barely masked his surprise. "Well . . . ah . . . thanks," he said.

"You didn't have to slash the tire on his new bike, though," the second kid said.

"Yeah, uncool," the first boy added.

Before Mark could deny it, the two boys turned and walked away.

Is this how it's going to be? Mark wondered. How could he be both a hero and a villain? He sighed and walked into Whit's End.

The sound of kids at play immediately gave Mark reassurance. He liked coming to Whit's End. Better still, he liked the friendly old inventor named John Avery Whittaker, or Whit, as he liked to be called.

He owned the place and was popular with everyone in town, especially the kids. It was easy to understand why. Whit was the kind of grown-up that let kids act like kids, but he talked and listened to them as if they were grown-ups. He made them feel important. Mark had figured this out for himself during the two weeks he worked for Whit as an errand boy.

Whit was behind the ice-cream counter, talking with Patti. Mark guessed by her dramatic gestures and facial expressions that she was retelling the events of that morning. Whit, a pleasant-looking man with unruly white hair and mustache, seemed to be listening with fascination. At times he smiled. Other times he frowned. In any case his face beamed with deep interest.

As Mark approached the counter, Whit and Patti turned

to him. Patti smiled in a way that made Mark feel uncomfortable. It was the kind of smile people made when looking at a litter of kittens.

"Hi, Mark," she gushed.

"Hi," Mark mumbled.

"There's a red lump next to your eye," she said proudly.

"I know," he answered with annoyance. *Good grief,* he thought.

"Sounds like you had a pretty tough morning," Whit said, his voice a rich, deep bass.

Mark nodded. "Yeah, I guess."

"You went home and changed clothes," Patti said.

Mark wondered why she was stating the obvious.

"So did I," she added.

Mark felt as if she were waiting for him to say something, but he wasn't sure what. "Oh," he finally said.

She frowned indignantly. "Don't you like it?"

Mark was puzzled. He looked to Whit for help. Whit, sensing the need, gestured to his shirt. Why his shirt? Mark was perplexed.

Whit tilted his head toward Patti's blouse.

Mark still didn't understand and finally gave up. "Like what?"

Whit put his hands over his face.

"My new blouse!" Patti sounded hurt. "You didn't notice."

"Oh that . . . ah, you know . . . I," Mark groaned.

Girls! he thought. *Doesn't she realize I have more important things to think about than a new blouse?*

Whit rescued the moment by changing the subject. "I guess you know we had a little mishap outside Whit's End today."

"Joe's slashed tire," Patti said.

"I didn't do it," Mark announced right away. "I went straight home after the fight. I didn't slash Joe's tire. Honest!"

Whit scrubbed his chin. "Hmm. Joe and his parents are convinced that you're the culprit."

"I don't care," Mark snapped. "I didn't do it."

"Then who did?" Whit asked.

"That's what I have to find out."

Patti was delighted. "We're going to solve a mystery!"

"We? Who said 'we'?" Mark challenged.

Patti was taken aback by his tone and stared at him, speechless.

"Now, Mark, every great detective needs an assistant," Whit said, his expression a mild rebuke.

Because it was Whit, Mark gave in. "Oh, all right."

Patti grinned.

"How are you going to start your investigation?" Whit asked.

Mark shrugged. "That's what I came to ask you. Where should I start?"

"Well, if you really want my help, I'd like to have a look

at that tire. Do you have it?"

"Joe's mom left it at my house. But, why?"

Whit shrugged, "Looking at the tire might tell us a few things, give us some clues."

"Okay, I'll bring it in. But what should I do?" Mark asked.

"What should *we* do?" Patti corrected him.

"What do you think you should do?" questioned Whit.

Mark thought for a moment and then exclaimed, "The scene of the crime! We should look for evidence outside at the bike rack. That's where it must have happened, right?"

Mark turned to go, but Patti stopped him. "Wait, Mark. The bike rack's no good."

"Why not?"

"Because everyone parks there. What kind of clues would you find after all this time?"

Mark grimaced. "Oh, that's right."

"Unless," Whit observed, "Joe didn't park his new bike at the bike rack."

Mark could tell Whit knew something. "What do you mean?"

"Maybe Joe is like a lot of people who get new cars. They don't park in the normal places. They park farther away so their new cars won't get bumped or scratched."

"Yeah?"

Whit grinned as he continued, "And maybe I took the

trash out earlier today and noticed that Joe's new bike was parked under the large oak tree away from the rest of the bikes."

"Maybe?" Mark smiled.

"Maybe."

Mark and Patti searched under the large oak behind Whit's End. The shade was surprisingly cool, considering the heat of the summer day.

Patti disappeared around the side of the tree. "See anything?"

"No, do you?"

"Nope." Patti reappeared. "Can you give me a hint about what we're looking for?"

"Clues!" Mark responded crossly.

"Don't talk to me like that," Patti snarled. "What kind of clues?"

"I don't know. Anything."

There was a soft thud against the side of the tree, and a pebble fell at Mark's feet. Joe stood a few yards away.

"I'm a good shot, and I could have hit you just as easy as I hit that tree," he said with a smirk.

Mark and Patti didn't answer but watched him silently.

"Looking for my bike so you can slash the other tire?"

"I didn't slash your tire," Mark said.

"Uh-huh," Joe answered with obvious disbelief. "Well, you better consider yourself warned, Mark-ee. I'm going to get you for what you did. Understand? Just watch yourself."

Joe kicked the dirt and walked away.

Patti started to go after him, but Mark took hold of her arm. "Don't, Patti."

Patti looked down at her arm and then up at Mark's face. She blushed. Mark pulled his hand away quickly.

"Come on," he said. "We aren't going to find anything around here."

Patti nodded and then suddenly looked down. "Wait," she said, kneeling. She picked up a small bracelet from the grass. "Do you think it's a clue?"

"I don't know. It might be," Mark said.

Patti held it up for both of them to see. The bracelet was made of two small chains with a wooden heart attaching them together. "It's kind of funny-looking, kind of like it was homemade."

Mark reached out for the bracelet. "Let me see."

In the middle of the wooden heart, written in an attempt at fancy script, was the name *Rachel.*

"Rachel!" Patti gasped.

"That's what it says." Mark shrugged. "Do you think it's your friend's?"

"There aren't a lot of Rachels in Odyssey. At least, not many who would lose a bracelet near Whit's End," she said, stopping to think about it a moment. "This is a weird place to lose a bracelet. I mean, it's not like people play around this tree very much."

Mark agreed. And he couldn't help but wonder if the same Rachel who had been picked on by Joe that morning had dropped the bracelet while she was slashing Joe's tire. Rachel seemed so nice, though.

Patti looked at Mark with concern. She must have guessed what Mark was thinking. "You don't think my friend, Rachel, slashed the tire, do you?"

Mark stared at the bracelet and said, "There's only one way to find out."

CHAPTER FOUR

Suspects

As Mark and Patti walked to Rachel's house, he thought about the bracelet and the questions it raised. If the bracelet were Rachel's, what was it doing under the tree? Had she dropped it while she was slashing Joe's tire? Was Rachel the kind of girl who would even slash a tire?

Mark turned to Patti and asked her if Rachel would do something like that.

Patti considered it for a moment and said, "I don't think so. We've been friends a long time, and I've never seen her act like that. She's quiet. If she's mad or upset, she goes home and eats some ice cream."

Mark recalled the surprising way Rachel shouted during the argument with Joe. "She sure yelled this morning," Mark said.

"So what? There's a big difference between yelling and slashing tires," Patti replied irritably.

"Then what was the bracelet doing there?" Mark asked.

"Maybe it's a coincidence." Patti grew more defensive. "Maybe it doesn't have anything to do with Joe's stupid bike!" She shoved her hands into her jeans pockets and stared at the sidewalk.

Mark didn't say anything else. *What's wrong with her?* he wondered. *Why is she being so moody?*

They arrived at Rachel's house not long after that. She was sitting on the top step of her front porch, eating ice cream. Mark noticed that her eyes looked red and puffy.

"How are you doing?" Patti asked when they reached her.

"I'm okay." Rachel shrugged.

"Joe's a jerk, Rachel. You know that," Patti offered.

"Yeah, I know."

"Mark and Joe got in a fight after you left. It was a whopper, too," Patti said proudly.

"Uh-huh," Rachel said and scooped a spoonful of vanilla ice cream into her mouth. Mark was getting hungry watching her.

Patti shuffled uncomfortably for a moment. When she spoke, she sounded stiff, as if she were trying to sound casual. "Um, have you . . . ah, you know . . . lost anything lately?"

Rachel looked up at Patti self-consciously. "You mean, weight?"

"No!" Patti said quickly. "I mean, like, jewelry or something like that."

Rachel thought about it and then shook her head no. "Not that I know of."

Patti continued, "I mean, like a necklace or bracelet maybe?"

Mark wished Patti would come right out and show Rachel the bracelet.

"I haven't lost anything, Patti. Why?" Rachel asked.

"Well . . . ah," Patti pulled the bracelet from her jeans pocket. "We found this today and figured it was yours. See? It has your name on it."

Rachel looked at the bracelet. For a second Mark thought her eyes widened. She quickly looked down and mumbled, "Nope. It's not mine."

Mark and Patti exchanged glances. Patti's expression seemed to ask, *What now?*

Mark sat on the step beneath Rachel's feet. "Are you sure?"

"I'm sure. I would know my own bracelet, wouldn't I?"

Mark nodded.

"Why? Is something wrong?" asked Rachel.

Patti looked to Mark. He explained what had happened since the morning: the fight, the slashed tire, his being accused and finding the bracelet where Joe parked his bike.

Rachel turned to Patti. "You thought the bracelet was mine, so you figured I slashed the tire! Is that why you're here? Thanks a lot, friend."

"It's not like that," Patti said apologetically. "We're just checking clues. Really."

"Oh, you're checking clues. So you're playing detectives now, huh? And I guess you automatically suspected the fat girl. They always do in the movies."

Mark tried to remember if the fat girls were always accused in the movies he had seen. He gave up when he couldn't think of any movies with fat girls in them. The ones in movies always seemed to be too thin and kept the hero from doing his job—kind of like Patti.

"Go pick on somebody else!" Rachel cried out. "I didn't slash Joe's tires. But I'm glad somebody did! Sometimes I wish he would move away or get in big trouble with the police, so they would arrest him or something." Her voice trailed to a mumble. Then, as an afterthought, she shrugged and added, "I don't even have a knife to slash his tires with."

Of course, Mark thought. *Why didn't I think of that before? Whoever slashed the tire must have been carrying a knife! Or if they weren't carrying one, they had to get one from somewhere. But where? Whit's End? Did the villain steal one of Whit's kitchen knives to do the job?*

"If you didn't slash the tire, who did? Who would want to?" Mark asked.

Rachel shrugged again. "Anybody who's ever been bugged by Joe. And that's most of the kids in Odyssey. He's a disgusting bully. He deserves to have more than his tire slashed."

"You got that right," Patti agreed. Shoving the bracelet back into her pocket, she said jokingly, "Maybe I did it, Mark."

Mark frowned at her. "Don't be stupid."

He turned his attention to Rachel again. "Can you think of someone else who would want to hurt Joe, someone Joe hurt recently? I can't talk to all the kids in Odyssey."

Rachel's expression made Mark suspect that she had thought of someone right away, but she didn't say it. She waited a moment and then reluctantly answered, "Well, there might be one person."

She paused dramatically. Growing more impatient, Mark began to gnaw at the inside of his lip.

"Chad Cox," she finally said.

"Chad!" Patti exclaimed. "Why would he want to hurt Joe? They're friends. He's been in the gang forever."

Rachel shook her head. "Not anymore. Something happened, and Chad got thrown out of the gang."

"What happened?" Mark asked.

"I don't know. Just . . . something happened." She stood slowly.

"But . . . but . . . ," Mark stammered. "If you know he got thrown out of the gang, you have to have some clue."

"You two are the hotshot detectives with all the clues," Rachel replied. "I have to go inside. Lunch is almost ready. See you guys later."

Once they were beyond Rachel's yard, Mark said, "Let's go back to my house and get the tire for Whit."

"Okay," Patti responded. She nonchalantly pulled the bracelet out of her pocket again and sighed. "Did you see it?"

"See what?"

"The way she looked when I asked if the bracelet was hers and she said 'no.' "

"What do you mean? What was I supposed to see?" Mark asked.

Patti held out the bracelet. "She was lying. This bracelet is hers."

CHAPTER FIVE

Pocketknives

Mark and Patti were a block away from Mark's house when Patti suddenly gasped, "There's Chad Cox."

Mark looked ahead and saw a blond-haired boy in overalls sitting on the curb. He was concentrating on something at his feet.

It was Mark's turn to be surprised. Chad Cox was the same blond-haired boy he had seen on the bike in the park, the one who had ridden after Rachel.

"I saw him at the park," Mark whispered.

"What?"

Mark signaled that he would tell her later. As they approached, Chad picked up the object at his feet. It was a small, half-finished wooden replica of a train engine. Chad pulled out a pocketknife and began whittling at the engine.

"He's got a pocketknife!" Patti whispered.

Mark nudged her to be quiet.

Chad slowly turned his head and looked up at them. He didn't acknowledge them in any way but went back to his whittling.

"Hi, Chad," Patti said, as she sat down next to him. "Do you know Mark?"

"I've seen him around," Chad replied. He spoke slowly in a soft monotone voice.

"Hi," Mark said, kneeling next to him on the other side. "That's a great-looking engine. Did you make it yourself?"

"Yep."

"You're pretty handy with a knife, huh? I guess you would have to be to make it look so real," Mark said, hoping to draw Chad out.

"I guess so," Chad responded.

"Where did you learn to whittle?" Patti asked.

"My daddy taught me."

They fell silent while Chad continued to work. Every once in a while he would stop to push his stringy, blond hair out of his face. Mark thought he could be good-looking if he scrubbed some of the dirt off his cheeks and wore some clothes without so many stains and holes.

"You and Joe are friends, aren't you?" Patti asked.

"Used to be."

"You're not anymore?" Patti pretended to be surprised.

"Guess you could say that."

"Boy, that's weird. How come you're not friends?"

Chad shrugged. "Just aren't, I guess."

Mark gritted his teeth. *This could take all day*, he thought.

"Did you hear about what happened to Joe's new bike?" questioned Patti.

"Somebody slashed the tire," Chad answered as he examined his engine. He blew the wood-dust off it and examined it closely again.

"Somebody thinks Mark did it," Patti explained, "and we're trying to prove he didn't."

"Uh-huh." Chad started whittling around the engine's smokestack.

"We thought you could help us," Patti went on.

Chad stopped whittling. For the first time, he looked full into Patti's and Mark's faces. "What makes you think I can help you?"

Mark said, "Because you had a falling out with Joe."

"So? Does that make me a tire-slasher?"

"No, but—"

"But you think I did it."

Mark eyed Chad more carefully. "Why did you and Joe stop being friends?"

"It's none of your business."

"Then how will we know you didn't slash the tire?" Patti reasoned. "You can tell us. Please, Chad? Anything you know might help crack this case."

Chad half-smiled, "Crack this case? You sound like one of those private whatevers on TV."

"All we want to do is find out who slashed the tire so Mark won't have to pay for it," Patti pleaded.

Mark was touched by her earnestness.

"I didn't slash anybody's tire," Chad said firmly.

"Okay, but why did you and Joe stop being friends?" Mark asked.

"I can't tell you," Chad responded, tightly gripping the engine. He knocked a sliver of wood away from it with his knife. "You'll laugh just like they did."

"We wouldn't laugh at you," Patti said assuringly.

"Yes, you would. You would laugh because you don't understand."

"Understand what?" Mark asked.

Chad looked at Mark and held the knife up like it was a finger. "You ever like a girl, Mark?"

Mark was taken aback. Like a girl? Did he mean like ooshy-gooshy holding hands or did he mean like a girl as a friend?

"Huh?" he replied.

"You know, have you ever liked a girl?"

Mark blushed slightly. It was the kind of question boys

asked each other only when they were good friends, only when they were talking seriously away from girls. Patti was staring at him with intense interest.

"What's that got to do with it?" asked Mark.

"It might have plenty to do with it," Chad said. "Well?"

Mark remembered a girl named Debbie back in Washington, D.C. He thought he liked her, but when she wrote a note to Karen saying that she liked a boy named Bob more than Mark, he decided he didn't like her after all. "I might have . . . once," Mark answered.

Patti smiled.

"I might have liked a girl once, too," Chad started to say and then fell into a thoughtful silence.

Mark and Patti waited. Mark felt sure Chad would open up and explain.

Chad took a deep breath and looked as if he might go back to whittling again. Then he put the engine on the pavement. "I didn't tell anybody I liked her. It was my own secret. I didn't even tell her for a long time. Then I told Joe because I thought we were friends. He laughed at me and told the rest of the gang. They wouldn't quit teasing me, so I left. I don't know why I ever hung out with them in the first place."

"Who did you like, Chad?" Patti asked quickly.

Chad was on guard again. "I told you enough." He picked up his wooden engine and carefully started carving again.

There wasn't a good reason to stay after that, so Mark and Patti said goodbye and walked on toward Mark's house.

"Okay, let's sort this out," Mark said. "There's this mysterious bracelet with Rachel's name on it that we found at the scene of the crime. And we know Rachel could have slashed the tire because Joe humiliated her this morning."

"And," Patti added, "even though she says the bracelet isn't hers, I think she might be lying."

"Why would she lie to us?"

"I don't know, but she is. I can tell."

"How can you tell?" Mark asked.

Patti glanced slyly at Mark and said, "Call it girl's intuition."

"We don't know where Rachel got the knife," Mark said, ignoring her comment. "Which brings us to Chad. He carries a knife. And he might have used it on Joe's tire because Joe laughed at him for liking a girl."

"But what girl?" Patti asked curiously.

"Rachel," Mark answered confidently.

"What?" Patti stopped and stared at Mark.

He was pleased. This reminded him of some of the detective stories he had read. He felt like Sherlock Holmes, with Patti as Dr. Watson.

"Are you nuts? You think Chad liked Rachel?"

"Not liked, he likes her."

I'm working into the role nicely, Mark thought.

"You're out of your mind," Patti scoffed.

Then Mark explained how he had seen a blond-haired boy on a bike at the park—Chad, in fact—follow Rachel after Joe teased her.

"A boy acts like that when he likes a girl," Mark said.

"Wow!" Patti's mouth gaped open.

"And that makes Chad a greater suspect," Mark added.

"It does?"

"Sure! If Chad has a crush on Rachel and saw how Joe picked on her, he might have slashed Joe's tire to get revenge for her."

Patti stared at Mark with amazement. "How did you figure all this out?"

"Elementary, my dear Patti," he smiled. "Elementary."

CHAPTER SIX

Peculiar Behavior

Mark and Patti picked up the slashed tire at his house and gave his mom an update on the case. She said they were doing a wonderful job, but Mark had the feeling she was only humoring them. He didn't understand why mothers didn't take such things more seriously.

"It's getting near suppertime," she said as they were leaving. "Be home soon. I may have a surprise for you."

Probably pizza, Mark guessed.

Back at Whit's End, Mark showed the tire to Mr. Whittaker. "What do you think?"

Whit turned the tire this way and that, examining the inside and outside of it before he answered. "It's a slashed tire, all right."

"Yeah, but can you figure any clues from it?" Mark tried to sound detective-like. Even though his reputation was at stake, he was beginning to enjoy the mystery.

"I'll need to do a few tests," Whit determined. "That's the only way to find out anything for sure. How is the rest of the case coming?"

Mark started to speak, but Patti interrupted and told Whit everything they had discovered. This annoyed Mark and made him wish Patti would go away. Dr. Watson should never interrupt Sherlock Holmes.

Whit stroked his chin again. He seemed particularly interested in the news about Chad and Rachel. "From what I saw on Friday," he said, "I don't think they are friends at all."

"Friday? What happened Friday?" Mark asked.

Whit brushed his finger lightly alongside his mustache. "Friday afternoon Chad was hanging around but not really doing anything. He acted like he was waiting for something or someone. When Rachel came in a little later, he was shy and nervous. Eventually, he talked to her, and they sat down together."

"You were right, Mark. It *is* Rachel he likes!" Patti exclaimed.

"Of course," Mark said.

Whit continued his account. "Chad and Rachel were in that booth," he said, gesturing toward one of them. "He had a soda, and she had a sundae. I thought it was nice that a boy and a girl can be friends, like you two," he smiled.

Patti blushed, and Mark rolled his eyes.

Whit continued, "Then it seemed like they were having a disagreement. She was looking very uncomfortable, and he was acting upset. She got up and walked out. A moment later, he followed her."

Mark put on his best thoughtful expression. "Hmm, curious."

"It concerns me when kids fight like that in my shop, so I walked outside to make sure everything was all right. I found them around the back by the oak tree. I didn't hear what was said, but I got there in time to see her throw something small at Chad and storm off. Chad saw me, became embarrassed and left in another direction. So much for boys and girls being friends, I thought." Whit smiled. "Well, Inspector? What do you make of it?"

Mark's voice was low and serious when he answered, "This makes it look worse for Chad. He's good with a knife and would have wanted to get revenge because Joe picked on Rachel. It's pretty simple."

"The bracelet!" Patti suddenly blurted. "That's why the bracelet was under the tree!"

Mark was confused. After playing the detective so well, he was ashamed to ask her why.

Whit asked instead, "Why was it there?"

"Because," Patti said proudly, "that's what you saw Rachel throw at Chad!" Patti dug in her pocket and held up the bracelet. "See the small wooden heart in the middle! I'll bet Chad made it for Rachel. He could have whittled it. And when they had that fight, she threw it at him!"

"Well done, Patti!" Whit exclaimed.

Mark reluctantly admitted, "You might be on to something."

"Might be! You know I'm right, Mark Prescott, and you're afraid to admit it," Patti scolded.

Mark scowled. "Okay, if you're so smart, tell me what they were fighting about."

She thought about it a moment and then shrugged it off. "It doesn't matter. Now we know why the bracelet was at the scene of the crime. Rachel didn't slash the tire."

"She still might have," Mark insisted.

"It's only circum . . . circum . . . ," Patti got stuck on the word and then said, "You know, that kind of evidence."

"If you mean it's only evidence that appears to be true because of the circumstances, but may not be true in fact, you mean 'circumstantial evidence,' " Whit explained.

"Thank you. It's only cir-cum-stantial evidence," Patti finished.

"But why did she lie about the bracelet?" Mark demanded.

"Where would she get a knife to slash a tire?" Patti countered.

Whit held up his hands. "All right, you two. That's enough. Some of these questions may be answered when

I get a good look at this tire."

Whit looked at his watch. "Your parents are probably wondering where you are. Go home for dinner, and we'll continue this later."

Walking through McAlister Park, Patti suddenly announced to Mark that she was going to walk him home. "I don't think you should go alone," she said.

Mark turned to her and asked, "Why not?"

"Because of Joe and his gang."

"What about them?" Mark asked.

"Joe said earlier he would get you for slashing his tire. He might be waiting around. I'm . . . I'm worried that he'll hurt you. I'll walk you home," she offered.

"I'm not going to have a girl walk me home. You think I can't handle Joe myself? He's after you, too, you know. I'll walk you home." Then Mark mumbled under his breath, "Dumb girl."

He noticed Patti smiling, and he wondered what she thought was so funny. Nearer to Patti's house, they began talking about Chad's crush on Rachel. Mark was wondering why, if Chad liked Rachel, he would get in a fight with her under the oak tree.

"Mark, you said you once liked a girl," Patti said. "Did you really?"

"Yeah, I did," he answered. He felt his cheeks turn warm.

"A lot?"

Mark growled, "Drop it, Patti. I don't want to talk about it."

"But . . . I think it's kind of cute."

"Cute!" Mark felt like his face had turned bright red.

"Yeah."

She had that same funny look again. It made Mark nervous. He tried to pick up their pace.

"Mark?" Patti ventured when they reached her front porch.

"What?"

"Did you ever . . . you know." Patti looked down at her feet shyly. "Did you ever kiss the girl you liked?"

"Are you off your rocker?" He looked around self-consciously, wondering if anyone else in the neighborhood heard the question.

"You mean, you liked her, but you never kissed her?"

Mark swallowed hard. "I . . . I have to go home, Patti."

"You could kiss me if you wanted to," Patti suddenly blurted.

"No way!" he replied, louder than he meant to.

Patti looked wounded. Her voice snapped back to its normal volume. "I wouldn't want you to kiss me anyway!"

With that, she turned and marched into the house. She slammed the door hard enough to make the front window rattle. Convinced that everyone in the neighborhood had gathered on their porches to see what the commotion was all about, Mark hurried off to the woods across the street.

The woods were dark. The thick leaves of the trees blocked what little light was given off by the slow summer dusk falling over Odyssey. Mark was doing his best to decide what in the world was wrong with Patti.

Why is she acting so strange? he wondered.

He pondered the question until he was deep in the woods, until he heard the crunching of leaves. His thoughts suddenly shifted from Patti to Joe.

Then Mark heard the sharp snapping sounds of branches breaking.

He spun around. The sounds suddenly stopped, but he couldn't see anything.

It's nothing, he thought.

The strange quiet told him otherwise, and he shuddered. He wished Patti hadn't reminded him of Joe's threats. It was like telling someone a horrifying monster story before going to bed.

Swish . . . swish . . . swish. It was the unmistakable rhythm of feet moving through leaves. Mark's heart began to pound. He jerked his head suddenly to the right, sure he saw something out of the corner of his eye.

"Is somebody there?" he called out feebly.

No one answered.

Frankly he wasn't sure he wanted an answer. What if it wasn't Joe? What if someone else were following him?

What would Sherlock Holmes do? Would he run?

Would he reason with the beast? Would he try to outwit it? Mark didn't know, and he didn't care to wait around for an answer. The shadows came alive, the sound of snapping branches and crunching leaves seemed close behind him. Mark started to run.

He thought he heard someone laugh. Or was it a cough? A growl? He ran faster, without looking back, following the path closely. He was racing as fast as his sneakers would take him. But the noises seemed to be keeping pace.

At last he reached the edge of the woods and broke into the brighter, though fading, sunlight. He wished he felt safer. His nerves wouldn't let him. If Joe or some sort of creature wanted to get him, it would be just as easy to get him in the street. Mark kept running, even though his legs were beginning to feel like two loose rubber bands.

He raced across his yard and went to the door closest to him, the one on the side of the garage. He pushed it open, his chest heaving from the effort. He slammed the door and collapsed against it. Clutching his aching side, he closed his eyes for a moment.

Slowly he reached up to the pane of glass in the door. Pushing the curtain aside, he peeked out to see if anything had followed him. Everything looked normal, even peaceful. He pressed his head against the glass to look down toward the woods.

There, on the barely shadowed edge, Mark saw something move. It was a dark figure. Mark blinked and looked again. He could see it. It wasn't a trick of his imagination. Something was moving around down there, watching, waiting—then suddenly it was gone.

Mark felt as though he would throw up and swallowed a couple of times to try and relax. He was home now and safe, he assured himself. Whatever was after him was down by the woods. It wouldn't dare come up here after him. No way. It wouldn't dare. Mark took a deep breath. It wouldn't dare.

Then he was grabbed from behind.

CHAPTER SEVEN

A Surprise Visit

Mark tried to scream, but he couldn't get a sound past the hand over his mouth. He struggled, but the strength of his captor was too great. Then he heard a gentle chuckle in his ear, very low, soft and familiar.

"That's for all those times you used to scare me when I was working in the garage," Richard Prescott said as he let go of his son.

"Dad!" Mark shrieked, leaping into his father's arms. They hugged for a moment that felt like forever.

Julie Prescott appeared at the doorway leading into the house and smiled as she watched them. "Did you find the box you were looking for, Richard?"

"I found more than that!" he answered and hugged

Mark again.

"I told you there might be a surprise for dinner," Mark's mom said.

Mark laughed. "I thought we were going to have pizza."

"I hope this is a little better than pizza. I drove all the way from Chicago to see you," his dad said as they walked into the kitchen.

"What are you doing here?" Mark asked, hoping this visit was a good sign of some sort.

His dad smiled. "I'm going to California on business, but before I go, I decided to come here. Only for the week-end, though."

Mark tried to disguise his disappointment. They hadn't seen each other for months, not since the family split up in the spring. Mark and his mother had moved to Odyssey and his father had stayed behind.

The marriage wasn't working out, Julie had told Mark. His parents needed time apart. He didn't understand then, and he wasn't sure he understood any better now. But he was glad to see his dad, if only for a weekend.

"Your mom's been telling me about Odyssey," his dad said. "You've been having some interesting adventures. You want to tell me about them?"

Mark grinned. In a flood of words, he unleashed all the facts and stories he had collected since arriving in Odyssey: Mr. Whittaker, Whit's End, Joe Devlin and the slashed tire.

Mark talked all the way through supper, ignoring the amused looks his mother and father exchanged. It took Mark back to the days when they were together and happy. He finished his Odyssey adventures with his race through the woods to get away from the mysterious pursuer.

Mark's father looked concerned. "Did you know about this, Julie?"

Mark's mom looked wide-eyed. "It's the first I've heard about it. It's not like Odyssey has a high incidence of crime. I haven't read of a single mugging or robbery since we moved here."

She turned to Mark. "Do you think it was Joe Devlin?"

Mark nodded. "It had to be. He said he was going to get me. Who else would chase me through the woods?"

"Maybe we should have a word with the Devlins," Julie suggested.

Richard Prescott pondered this a moment. "Maybe we should," he said. Then he tossed his napkin on the table and smiled. "Well, I want you and your mom to give me a full tour of Odyssey tomorrow, okay?"

Mark looked to his mom for approval.

"After church," she said.

"Yeah!" Mark shouted.

Richard Prescott reached for his wife's hand, but she moved it away self-consciously.

"Mark," his mother said softly, "your father and I want

you to know that . . . that..." It was as much as she could say. Her eyes filled with tears, and she put her head down.

A tight grip of fear seized Mark's stomach. *What now?* he wondered. *Are they getting a divorce? Is this the big announcement?*

He stared intently into his father's face. It was set in a determined expression, but the eyes were sad.

His father cleared his throat nervously. "Son, I know this separation has been hard for you. It's tough to understand what's going on. We don't want to make things worse than they've been. But we don't want to give you any false hope."

False hope? Mark wondered what he meant.

His dad's eyes were teary, causing Mark's to water. "I've been an idiot. I . . . I'm not sure what I was thinking. I'm not sure how we're going to do it, but . . . ," Mark's father took his mother's hand again, and this time she wrapped it with hers. "But your mother and I want to get help. We want to see if we can give our marriage another try. I want to be part of the family again."

Mark's mouth fell open.

"Do you think you can forgive me enough to let me do that?" his father asked as large tears rolled down his ruddy cheeks.

Mark fell into his dad's arms and cried. Julie joined in, the three of them hugging and crying at the dining room table. It was the only answer Mark could give.

Then the phone rang, once, twice and several more times before his mother pulled herself away to get it.

"It won't be easy," his dad said, stroking Mark's hair. "We have a lot of things to work out, a lot of things to decide. But we'll get counseling. Your mother thinks the pastor can help us." He kissed Mark on the top of the head. "I don't know how I thought I could live without you."

Julie returned to the dining room. She was visibly shaken.

"Julie? Is everything all right?" Richard asked, rising from his chair.

She dabbed at her eyes with a tissue. "That was Mrs. Devlin, Joe's mother."

Mark looked up and cried out, "We can't pay her until I find out who really did it! Why is she bugging us?"

Julie shook her head. "That wasn't why she called. Apparently Joe got beat up in the woods on his way home this evening. She says she's going to call the police if we don't come right over."

"Joe was attacked in the woods!" Mark said with surprise. "But what does it have to do with me?"

"Mark," his mother said, "Mrs. Devlin thinks you did it."

CHAPTER EIGHT

A Bullied Bully

The Devlins' house was a sprawling, run-down Victorian on the south end of Main Street, right where the shops and office buildings ended and a residential section began. An electric red-and-white pole with a barber sign was on the street. A small stairwell led to the basement of the house, where Mr. Devlin had his barbershop.

The Prescott family walked past the pole and the stairwell to the front porch steps. Mrs. Devlin was waiting at the door. Her expression was stern and unyielding.

She led them to the living room where Joe sat on the couch, his head tilted back to balance the ice pack on his eye. Alan, Joe's younger brother, stood nearby and seemed fascinated by all the fuss. He flitted around nervously until Mrs. Devlin told him to sit down and be still. They were all informed that Mr. Devlin was in the basement with a late-evening customer.

"I didn't call the police," Mrs. Devlin said. "I thought we could work this out ourselves as civil and mature adults. I know you must feel terrible having a juvenile delinquent for a son."

Richard Prescott protested, "Excuse me, Mrs. Devlin, but I'm not sure we have enough facts to know that Mark did this to Joe."

Mrs. Devlin looked surprised. "What do we need? Mark has been terrorizing my Joe all day. First the fight, then the tire, now this!" She folded her arms. "Maybe I should have called the police. I didn't believe you would have the nerve to come here and deny it!"

Mark's father spoke calmly. "Why don't we hear Joe's story? Then we'll see whether you should call the police. Joe? Can you tell us what happened?"

Joe leaned forward, letting the ice pack drop into his hand. His left eye was a deep red and was turning black and blue. Apart from that, he looked like he always did—angry.

"I took a shortcut through the woods to get home," he explained. "Somebody jumped me and gave me this black eye."

"Not somebody," Mrs. Devlin corrected him. "Mark.

Didn't you say it was Mark who did it? Remember when you came home?"

Joe looked up at Mr. and Mrs. Prescott, his resolve floundering. "Well, no. *You* said it was Mark, Mom. You said it couldn't be anybody else."

"You didn't actually see who jumped you?" Mark's father asked.

"No, I got jumped from behind. If it was face to face, I wouldn't have this black eye. I would have won. I always win in a fair fight," Joe insisted.

"How long ago did this happen?" asked Julie Prescott.

"About a half hour ago," Joe answered.

Mr. Prescott held up his hands. "Well, Mark couldn't have done it then."

Mrs. Devlin looked at them suspiciously. "Why not?"

"Because he's been home with us for the past hour," Mark's father replied.

Mrs. Devlin sneered. "That's exactly what I would expect you to say—anything to cover for your son."

Richard Prescott looked intently into her face. "Mrs. Devlin, I don't think you know us well enough to judge whether we would lie for our son or not."

"All parents lie for their children," she said.

"Do you?"

"Well . . . , " Mrs. Devlin stopped, realizing the trap she had fallen into.

Mr. Prescott went on, "If Mark has done something

wrong, he'll be punished. But, in this case, I promise you that he was home with us when Joe was attacked. In fact, he was afraid someone was following him in the woods, too."

"So he was in the woods!" Mrs. Devlin exclaimed. "And so was my Joe."

"Yes, but that was an hour ago," Mr. Prescott answered. "Maybe the same person who chased after Mark also hurt Joe."

As Mark looked at Joe, he came to an unexpected realization.

"How long were you in the woods?" Mark asked.

"I told you; it happened half an hour ago. I was taking a shortcut home," Joe snapped back.

"A shortcut from where?" Mark asked.

"What are you, some kind of lawyer? I was coming home from . . . ," He paused for a second and then said, "Whit's End."

"You took a shortcut through the woods from Whit's End? But it's shorter through the park. You would have to go out of your way to go through the woods."

"I don't know," Joe stammered. "I'm . . . I'm confused. Maybe I was coming from somewhere else. I don't remember."

"It was only a half hour ago, Joe. You must remember where you were," Mr. Prescott said.

"Mom, tell them to quit asking so many questions. My

eye hurts!" Joe cried.

"That's enough," Mrs. Devlin said, rushing to her son's side. "He's the victim, not the culprit. You won't turn this on him!"

Joe laid his head back, and his mother placed the ice pack on his eye.

"You were the one who chased me in the woods, weren't you?" Mark asked Joe. "That's why you were coming home through the woods. It's a shortcut from *my* house, not Whit's End."

Joe jerked himself up, yanked the ice pack from his eye and shouted, "I told you what happened! I was taking a shortcut home from Whit's End when someone jumped me from behind. We wrestled in the dark and then *she* hit me!"

"She?" Julie asked.

Joe stumbled over his words, "She. He. It. Whatever it was. I couldn't tell. But that's how it happened! If you don't believe me, that's your tough luck."

Mrs. Devlin urged Joe to sit back and then whispered, "It's all right, Joseph. Calm down."

She put the ice pack on his eye again and turned to the Prescotts. "See what you've done? You've upset him."

Sitting there with his frail face, black eye and ice pack, Joe looked weak.

He's not so tough, Mark thought. *He's a scared kid just like me.*

Mr. Prescott gestured for Mark to come along and then addressed Mrs. Devlin. "You can call the police if you want, Mrs. Devlin. I don't think they'll be able to help you, though."

The Prescotts let themselves out into the warm summer night. On the front porch, Mark could hear Mrs. Devlin in the living room. "How could you be so stupid!" she screamed at Joe. "You're going through the woods. You're coming from Whit's End. Why don't you get your story straight? You humiliate me! We'll see if your father has something to say about this—with a razor strap! Now, go to your room!"

"Ow, Ma. Don't! Let go of my arm!" Joe protested.

Mark could also hear Alan laughing and wondered if he would do the same if he had an older brother who got in trouble. For the first time, Mark felt sorry for Joe.

Rocko loves Delores
AL + HK
BILLY loves SUZIE
PATTI + MARK 4EVER
J.D. + P.J.
P.S. loves T.Z.

CHAPTER NINE

An Initial Clue

Mark found it hard to concentrate on the sermon in church.

For one thing, he was excited that his father was with them. For the other, he was trying to piece together the clues surrounding Joe's slashed tire and the black eye someone had given him in the woods.

Considering all the enemies Joe seemed to have, it could have been anyone. Rachel? She had her own reason to want to hurt Joe. Her bracelet had been found at the scene of the crime, but could she have given Joe a black eye? It didn't seem possible.

Chad had the motive, and he had a knife. He could have easily been in the woods and attacked Joe. Maybe there was someone else Mark didn't know about, someone who had it in for Joe? Mark slumped in the pew. If that were true, then he might never find out who did it. One way or another, Mark had to discover who was doing these things to Joe Devlin. Otherwise he would be stuck with the blame and have to pay for the tire.

After the church service ended, Mark looked for Whit so he could introduce his father. He also wanted to tell Whit the latest news about what had happened to Joe Devlin in the woods. But Whit had already left.

"You two should have time alone," his mother said to Mark and his dad after they returned home and changed clothes. "I've fixed some sandwiches for a picnic. Why don't you go up to Trickle Lake for a while?"

She gave Mark's dad an awkward kiss before they left. Until then, Mark had forgotten how long it had been since he had seen them show any affection.

Mark and his father climbed into Mr. Prescott's rental car and drove through the picturesque mountain roads to one of the most beautiful spots in the area: Trickle Lake. On one end, it offered a view of Odyssey itself. On the other end, it was surrounded by paths leading into the adjoining hills and mountains. The people of Odyssey treasured it for its clean water, good fishing and general quietness.

Mark and his father ate and then threw a baseball around for a while. Then they hiked along the shadowed paths of the forest. Mark knew them because of Patti; they had wandered there together a few times. He pointed out The Great Tree, supposedly the tallest tree in the county. It was said that whoever could climb to the top of the tree would see cities in three surrounding states. Neither Mark nor his father was in the mood to find out if it were true.

"Patti said she climbed the tree once," Mark said, "but I'm not sure I believe her."

His father chuckled. "I've been meaning to ask you about this Patti you keep talking about. Does my son have a girlfriend?"

"No!" Mark thundered. "She just likes to hang around me, that's all."

"Come on, Mark. This is your dad you're talking to. You can tell me man-to-man."

"Cut it out, Dad!"

"Maybe one of these trees has your initials, huh?" He laughed and moved to the side of the path, where several trees were scarred with a variety of carvings. Outlined by the brown bark, the hearts with arrows through them, initials and names were a lighter tan. At the base of one tree, a small sign said it was the Lover's Tree and noted that many of the carvings went as far back as the middle 1800s, when Odyssey was first established.

Mark frowned and tugged at his dad's sleeve. "Come on, Dad. Let's go."

His dad waved for him to wait. "I want to look at some

of these older inscriptions. Maybe it'll give me inspiration for your mom."

Mark shuffled his feet and glanced at the tree-trunk carvings: Billy Loves Suzie. Rocko & Delores. J.D. + P.J.

Pretty stupid stuff, Mark thought. Then he did a double take when his eye caught one particular carving. He moved closer to make sure it said what he thought it did. To his horror, it read: Patti & Mark 4 Ever. It was in the middle of a perfectly rounded heart. Mark groaned.

Mark's dad was at his shoulder now. "Well, well, well," he said. "What do we have here? Ah, it looks fresh. And it's so artistically done."

Mark walked away. *Patti!* he fumed to himself. *Why did she do such a thing? I never said I liked her! Now everyone in Odyssey will think we're boyfriend and girlfriend!*

He kicked a small stone that spun into the woods and muttered aloud, "I never want to talk to her again!"

"Are you sure there isn't more to your relationship with Patti than you've told me?" his dad teased.

"She's really weird, Dad," Mark responded. "She started following me around when we first moved here. Everyone teased me. I mean, I didn't want a girl for a friend anyway, but . . . but she kept coming around."

"I think it's good for boys to have girls as friends," his dad observed.

Mark recalled that Mr. Whittaker had said the same thing, but it didn't make him feel any better.

"Everything was okay," Mark continued. "When we did things together, I kind of forgot she was a girl because she's good at sports and knows how to play army and . . . well, she's fun. But lately she's been acting funny."

"What do you mean by funny?"

Mark screwed up his face as he tried to explain. "She got all upset because she woke up with a pimple yesterday morning. Then she kept looking at me with this goofy expression. And she got mad because I didn't say how nice her clothes were."

Mr. Prescott began to chuckle.

"And . . . and . . . she asked me to kiss her!"

Mark's dad laughed heartily. He pulled his son closer and gave him a hug. "What a terrible thing to suffer through."

"You're telling me! I don't know what her problem is," Mark cried out.

"Patti's problem, if it's a problem at all, is simple," his dad explained. "She's becoming a young woman."

Mark grimaced. "Oh, brother."

His father shrugged. "It happens eventually. Didn't we have this little talk before?"

"You mean about the birds and the bees and the storks and stuff?"

"Well, yes."

"I think the whole thing is disgusting," Mark said. "And if Patti is starting to get like that, she's going to have to find a new friend. I'm not interested."

"Son, don't lose a good friend over something like this. Friends are to be valued like family whether they're boys or girls. Just be patient while she goes through these changes."

Mark wasn't sure he agreed but nodded anyway.

"Besides," his father added, "she may grow up and make a lot of money as a woodworking artist."

Mark didn't know what he meant.

His father pointed to the tree. "Look at the way she carved your names in this tree. She shows a lot of dexterity with a knife."

"Dexterity?" Mark asked.

"Dexterity means 'skill,' " Mr. Prescott explained. "It means she's good at using a knife."

Mark looked at the carving and had to agree. It was well-done, certainly not like the other scrawls. But Patti had never told Mark she was good with a knife. Why hadn't she?

By the time he and his father returned to Odyssey, Mark had new suspicions about who might have slashed Joe's tire.

CHAPTER TEN

A Confession

On the way home from Trickle Lake, Mark took his father to Whit's End. He hoped Mr. Whittaker might be around, even though it was closed Sundays. Whit wasn't to be found, and Mark was disappointed.

"I'll have to meet your Mr. Whittaker friend next time," his dad said.

Mark was pleased to hear there would be a next time. Any mention of his parents' future together helped him believe they really could be a family again.

Back home, Julie informed Richard that she had talked to the pastor about counseling. The pastor said he could meet with them for a short time in the afternoon. Mark sensed that his mother and father needed to be alone for a while, so he decided to go visit Patti. This was his chance to ask her a few new questions about the slashed tire.

He took the shortcut through the woods again. In the daylight Mark wondered why he had let himself become as frightened as he had. Then he remembered the dark figure on the edge of the woods.

He hurried to the Eldridges's house and waited on the veranda while Patti's mother went to get her. Even though it was late in the afternoon, the day was still bright and alive. Mark closed his eyes and listened to a distant lawn mower, the neighbor children laughing, a passing bike with a card in the spokes and a slamming screen door that announced Patti's arrival.

Mark looked up as Patti sat down next to him. She was wearing a delicate pink dress Mark assumed she had left on from church. She kept her gaze away from his, looking ahead to the front lawn or down at her tightly clenched hands. A knuckle on her right hand was scraped. Her hello was awkward and her manner distant.

This wasn't the Patti Eldridge Mark had become friends with over the summer. This was the Patti with a new dress and a pimple on her forehead, who had asked him to kiss her the evening before. This was the Patti who had carved a heart and two names in a tree at Trickle Lake.

Do I really know her? Mark questioned. *No, I don't.*

Yet this was the same Patti who could have slashed

Joe's tire. Exactly why, Mark wasn't sure. He wished he had stayed home. He didn't want to be with this new Patti. He didn't know how to talk to her. What would Sherlock Holmes do?

"My dad's here to visit," Mark said. Sherlock Holmes probably wouldn't talk about his dad, but it was the only thing Mark could think to say.

"Yeah, I know. I saw him in church this morning," replied Patti.

A moment of silence passed between them.

Then Mark asked, "Did you hear about Joe getting punched?"

Patti shook her head. "No, what happened?"

"He said he was walking through the woods on his way home last night and somebody jumped him from behind. His mother thought I did it and called us up. We went over to their house, and Joe was sitting on the couch with an ice pack on his face. He looked terrible."

Patti smiled slightly. "Really?"

"Yeah!" Mark said. "He had the biggest fat lip I've ever seen. It was funny-looking."

Patti looked perplexed. "You mean black eye."

A bird screeched and flew from the roof above them. Mark spoke softly, "I thought you didn't know about it."

"I didn't," she said.

"Then how did you know it was his eye instead of his lip?" Mark asked. He thought it was a trick worthy of

Sherlock Holmes, but he didn't feel good about it. It was like catching Dr. Watson stealing money from his desk.

Patti's cheeks reddened. "You . . . you said it was his eye."

"No, I didn't."

"Yes, you. . . ," Patti stopped. Her face suddenly went very tight, and Mark thought she might cry. She tugged at her dress and turned her head away. "You're right. I punched Joe."

"Why?"

She turned to face him again. "Because!" she snapped. "I know Joe better than you do. He's been picking on me for years. He said he was going to hurt you, and I figured he would try it when you were walking home last night. After you left my house, I followed you through the woods."

"That was you? You were the one who scared me half to death?"

"No, you idiot! That was Joe!" she shouted. "I told you he would do it. But you wouldn't listen to me, so I followed you, and I saw Joe, Alan, Lance and a few others. I saw them chase you in the woods. It made me mad. After you ran into your garage, I followed them back to see what they were going to do next. Joe and Alan got in a fight, and Joe made him go home. Then the rest of the gang sat around and laughed at you. I was really mad, so when they split up, I followed Joe and jumped on him."

Now Mark understood why Joe had accidentally said "she" when he told his side of the story. That's why he hadn't confessed. He was too ashamed to admit a girl had given him a black eye.

Patti sighed deeply. "Are you going to tell?"

"No," Mark said, pausing to think about it. "But *you* should. Right?"

She looked sadly at Mark and nodded in agreement. Then she began to cry. Slowly, at first, with a slight quiver of her bottom lip and a film of water over her eyes. Then the telltale sniffles came, quickly followed by tears sliding onto her cheeks.

Mark didn't know what to do. Something inside told him to put his arm around her, but it was broad daylight. They were on the front porch, after all. What should he do? Patti settled it by springing up and running inside.

Mark walked home feeling like a rat. He hated to make a girl cry.

But he still puzzled over the most important question. Since she had punched Joe, had she slashed his tire, too?

Mark reached his front lawn and saw his mother and father standing in the driveway. They were next to the rental car, talking intensely, oblivious of Mark. Then they hugged each other. His father was leaving.

"Dad!" Mark called out as he ran to them. "Where are you going?"

"Work. I've been waiting for you," his dad said, pulling

his son close. "I thought you were going to make me miss my plane."

"But you can't go! I thought you were leaving tomorrow."

"I'm going to California tomorrow, but I have to drive back to Chicago tonight. I'm glad you got here in time. I promised myself I would never leave you again without saying goodbye first," he said, giving Mark a squeeze.

"But you can't go," Mark said weakly.

Richard Prescott held his son at arm's length and looked him square in the eye. "I'll be back, Mark. I promise."

They hugged again; then he hugged Mark's mom, climbed into the car and drove away. They watched until the car reached the end of the street. His dad tapped the horn and disappeared around the corner. Now it was Mark's turn to cry.

STATION

CHAPTER ELEVEN

New Evidence

Monday morning, Whit didn't even have time to turn around the Whit's End Open sign before Mark arrived. Whit listened with great interest as Mark told him about his dad's visit and his parents' counseling and about Joe's black eye and Patti's confession. He also explained his latest suspicions. When Mark finished, Whit gestured for him to follow him to the basement.

Whit's workroom, a room Mark knew well, was cluttered with odd-shaped gadgets and half-finished inventions. The Imagination Station sat in the center, a large and imposing machine. Mark touched it affectionately as he walked past it to the workbench. Joe's slashed tire and a large microscope were sitting on the bench. The tire looked more mangled than before.

"I checked the tire for clues," Whit said with flourish. "Climb up on this stool and look through the microscope. I have a piece of the tire under there."

Mark pressed his eyes against the double lens and focused the microscope. A black mass of tire came into view.

Whit guided him along. "You see the tire?" he asked. "Notice the edge of it on the right side there. What do you see?"

Mark could make out the bumps of the tread, which were mountainous through the magnifier. He then noticed the interruption where the clean edge of the slash had been made.

"All I see is a slashed tire," Mark confessed.

Whit chuckled. "But take a good close look at that slash and I'll show you something else. Don't move."

Mark watched through the lens as Whit removed the piece of tire. Bright light replaced it for a moment, and then Whit slid what looked like the same piece back under the lens.

"I tried a little experiment with a tire of the same make," Whit said. "Do you see a difference?"

Mark could see the bumps of tread beside the slash mark. But this time the slash mark was ragged and frayed. It wasn't sharp and straight like the first one.

"This is different!" Mark exclaimed.

Whit patted Mark's shoulder. "Good. Because the second tire was slashed with a regular pocketknife with a normal blade. It's the kind of knife Chad would use to whittle with or Patti might use to carve initials in a tree. Even a kitchen knife makes a similar kind of slash."

Mark felt embarrassed. "I don't get it," he admitted.

"It means that Chad or Patti would have had to use a much sharper knife to slash Joe's tire. A knife requiring a very special kind of blade."

Mark stared at Whit, puzzled.

"I think we should call all the suspects and have them meet us here," Whit said with a smile. "I think we've reached the end of this case."

CHAPTER TWELVE

The Case Is Solved

When Mark and Whit entered Whit's office, everyone involved in the case was waiting for them. Patti was sitting off by herself, tugging uncomfortably at her blue-and-white-patterned dress. Chad was standing nearby, his hands shoved deep into his overalls. He had the same blank expression he always seemed to have. Rachel was sitting by the opposite wall.

Mrs. Devlin, Joe and Alan were sitting together on the visitors' couch. Joe's eye had turned a light shade of bluish-red. Alan couldn't seem to sit still, so Mrs. Devlin pinched him.

"Too much boyish energy," she said to Whit.

Mark wished Mrs. Devlin hadn't come. But when Whit

called, she had taken the phone from Joe and insisted that she be there.

"Well?" Mrs. Devlin said impatiently. "What's this big secret you're keeping? I can't wait to see how Mark has weaseled his way out of this one."

"I didn't weasel my—" Mark began.

Whit touched Mark's arm to silence him and moved to the center of the group. "Since we're not the police or lawful authorities," he said calmly, "I thought it would be best to settle this case quietly among those involved. I didn't see any sense in making a big fuss out of it."

Mrs. Devlin scoffed, "Oh, that's right. Protect the guilty one! Well, I'll be the one to say whether the police will be involved or not." She glared at Mark.

Whit gestured to Mark and said, "It's all yours, inspector."

Whit sat down behind his desk as Mark stepped forward nervously and cleared his throat. "Thanks, Mr. Whittaker. I know you've all been wondering about this case since you're involved in it one way or another. It's taken a few twists and turns since the beginning and—"

"Get on with it!" Joe growled. "You think this is a movie or something?"

Mark stopped, stammered a little and then continued in a detective-like tone. "Okay. Let's go through it one step at a time. Somebody slashed the tire on Joe's new bike. A few people thought it was me because Joe and I had a fight earlier. It so happens that I wasn't the only one who had had a run-in with Joe. Lots of people in Odyssey seemed to have a reason to slash Joe's tire. I've narrowed it down to a handful. The fact is, it was someone in this room."

Everyone looked around suspiciously.

"You think I did it?" Patti asked, injured. "Thanks a lot!"

"You could have, Patti," Mark stated. "You and Joe do a lot of fighting. But that wasn't the only reason you were a suspect. I also saw some of the carving you did on a tree at Trickle Lake." Mark gritted his teeth as he mentioned it.

Patti blushed. "So? I was just playing around. It was a joke."

"But it showed me you can be real handy with a knife. Slashing Joe's tire would have been easy for you. You had enough motives. You could have slashed Joe's tire because he picks on you or because he picked on Rachel that morning or for other reasons. We know you and Joe had a fight Saturday night."

"What?" Joe bellowed.

"In the woods, Joe," Mark said. "You know as well as I do that it was Patti who punched you in the eye. You knew it all along. You didn't say so because you didn't want anyone to know a girl gave you a black eye."

Alan made a snorting sound.

Patti rose to her defense. "I did it because Joe and his

gang scared you in the woods, and it made me mad. He deserved a black eye."

"Is that true?" Mrs. Devlin shouted at Joe.

Joe sank further into the couch's cushions. "Yeah, but that was to get back at Prescott. We were just having fun."

"And you let this girl give you a black eye?" Mrs. Devlin demanded. "Wait until your father hears about this!"

"Aw, Ma," Joe whined.

Mrs. Devlin turned to Patti. "Then you slashed my son's tire."

"No!" Patti cried out. She faced Mark. "Did you think I would let you take the blame for slashing Joe's tire if I did it? I . . . I thought we were friends."

"We are, Patti," Mark said.

"Aw, isn't that sweet," Joe mocked.

"Patti didn't do it, Mrs. Devlin," Mark stated.

"Oh, yes. I'm going to believe you after that little love scene? If she didn't, who did?" Mrs. Devlin gestured to Chad, who was leaning passively against the wall. "Was it Mr. Overalls over there? He's always walking around whittling things with that pocketknife of his."

Chad looked down self-consciously at his pocketknife.

"I wondered the same thing," Mark said, resuming his detective-like tone. "He certainly had the right kind of weapon, and his motive was even better. Revenge."

Chad straightened his shoulders. "This isn't anybody's

business."

Mark pleaded, "Do you want everyone to think you did it?"

Chad thought about it and then slumped against the wall again. "I don't care. It doesn't matter much any-more."

"What's all this nonsense? What are you talking about?" Mrs. Devlin snarled.

Mark paced slowly in front of a large bookcase. "When Patti and I first checked the scene of the crime—"

"Come on, Prescott, stop trying to be so tough. What scene of the crime?" Joe taunted.

"The tree where you parked your bike," Mark returned. "We found a small bracelet there. It had a wooden heart and the name Rachel carved on it. We thought Rachel had dropped it. But she later denied it was hers. It didn't make sense. Why would she lie about her bracelet?" Stabbing the air with his finger, he said, "Unless Rachel slashed the tire and dropped the bracelet by accident."

Rachel turned to Mark, her eyes wide with horror.

Mrs. Devlin frowned. "Rachel? Why in the world would she want to do that?"

"Because Joe teased her that morning about being," Mark tried to find the right word and then said, "A little overweight."

"Fat! She's fat! Why don't you just say it?" Joe shouted.

Rachel lowered her head.

Mrs. Devlin pinched his arm. "Shut up, Joe! You're in enough trouble as it is."

"But Rachel didn't do it," Mark explained. "For one thing, she's not the sort of person who would hurt Joe or his tire. For another thing, the bracelet really wasn't hers."

Patti looked surprised. "It wasn't?"

Mark shook his head. "Nope."

"Then whose was it?" asked Patti.

Mark paused for full effect. "Chad's."

All eyes turned to Chad, whose face turned red.

Mark kept talking. "Chad made it for Rachel because he liked her. You knew about that, Joe. That's why Chad left the gang."

"You can't like girls and be in my gang," Joe said simply. "Especially not girls like—"

Joe squealed when Mrs. Devlin pinched him again.

"Finish your story, Prescott," she said.

"Chad tried to give the bracelet to Rachel under the oak tree. But she didn't feel the same way about Chad and told him so. Chad got mad. Maybe he said a few things he didn't mean to say. He told her to keep the bracelet, but she didn't want it. Rachel threw the bracelet at him and walked away. He left it on the ground. On Saturday Joe parked his bike under the same tree. And the bracelet was still there when his tire was slashed. Isn't that right,

Chad?"

Chad shrugged. "You're the detective."

"And my guess," Mark continued, "is that Chad was trying to find Rachel in the park Saturday morning to apologize. That's when Joe teased her so much she went home crying. Chad saw what happened, and he was steamed about it. That's why I thought he'd slashed the tire."

Mrs. Devlin turned to Chad. "Okay, Mr. Overalls, I think you owe us some money."

Chad opened his mouth to speak, but Mark interrupted. "That would be true, Mrs. Devlin, if it were Chad. But it wasn't."

"Good grief," Mrs. Devlin groaned. "Are you going to give us the life story of everyone in Odyssey before you get to the bottom of this? I'm still not convinced you're innocent, you know. And if you're guilty, I might just make you pay me for all this time you're wasting."

Mark moved back toward Whit. "Just one more thing, Mrs. Devlin. Whit examined the tire and discovered that it wasn't slashed with an ordinary pocketknife or even a kitchen knife. It was slashed with a special kind of blade."

Mrs. Devlin shook her head impatiently. "Why should I care what kind of blade slashed the tire?"

"Because you might recognize it," Whit said, leaning forward in his chair. He held up the object Mark had seen on the workbench.

"A straight razor?" Mrs. Devlin blinked.

"This was my father's," Whit said as he carefully pulled the stainless steel blade from its cover. "He used to shave with it every morning. It's extremely sharp. Of course, most men don't shave with straight razors anymore. They use the disposable kind. These days you'll usually find straight razors being used in one place."

Whit paused, and everyone remained quiet as they waited for him to tell them where. Mrs. Devlin already knew and had turned pale.

"A barbershop," Whit said.

"Just like Mr. Devlin's barbershop," Patti gasped.

Mrs. Devlin's tone of voice turned to a vicious growl. "What are you saying, Mr. Whittaker? You think my husband slashed my son's tire?"

"Of course not," replied Whit.

"I didn't do it!" Joe cried out.

"I certainly didn't," snapped Mrs. Devlin.

Rachel asked quietly, "Then who did?"

Mark and Whit both looked at the culprit. One by one, the rest of the group did the same.

"Alan?" Patti cried out.

Alan's eyes darted back and forth as he curled up on the couch. It seemed as if he wanted to shrink into the fabric itself.

"Alan!" Mrs. Devlin screamed.

"I . . . I . . . ," Alan stuttered.

"Did you slash Joe's tire?" Mrs. Devlin asked, pressing her face closer to Alan's.

His mouth moved without forming any words; then he scrunched his face into a frown. "Joe yells at me in front of the gang and makes me feel stupid. And you got him a new bike and wouldn't get me one. And I hate him! He's the worst brother in the world!"

With an indignant roar, Mrs. Devlin was on her feet in an instant. Her face was a patchwork of reds, purples and violets. She grabbed one of Alan's ears and one of Joe's. "Home! This minute! Both of you! I've never been so . . . so just wait until your father . . . you're going to regret the . . ."

Chad opened the door for them, and she stormed out with her boys yelping the whole way down the stairs. They could be heard muttering and screaming all the way through Whit's End and out onto the sidewalk in front.

"Whew!" Mark sighed.

"It's heartbreaking," Whit observed. "It's bad enough when strangers try to hurt each other. Somehow it seems worse when it happens between brothers."

Everyone nodded silently.

Whit stood and said, "Maybe they'll learn something from this. Maybe we all will."

Mark recalled how it had felt to be at the Devlins the night he was accused. He remembered Mrs. Devlin yelling at Joe. Then Mark thought about the time Joe had yelled at Alan. One person bullying another person who bullies yet another. Mark wondered how a home could become so full of anger and jealousy.

"You can go now, if you want," Whit announced, "or you can stick around for some free ice cream. It seems the least I can do after all this."

Chad declined the offer and moved toward the door.

Mark caught him before he could go. "I'm sorry, Chad," Mark said. "I hope you're not mad at me."

Chad shrugged. "Nah, you great detectives have to get your cases solved, don't you?"

Chad turned and strolled out of the office.

Rachel said to Whit, "I would have some ice cream, but I just had some."

As she hurried out the door, Mark thought he heard her call Chad's name.

"Well done, detective Prescott!" Whit said proudly, thumping Mark on the back.

"You were the one who solved it," Mark responded.

"Not at all. You and Patti put together most of the pieces." Whit gave Mark's shoulder a gentle squeeze and walked over to Patti, who was still in her chair. "It was nice of you to dress up for the occasion, Patti. Doesn't she look lovely in that dress, Mark?"

Patti looked up at Mark expectantly.

"Yeah," he said. "It's pretty, I guess. But will it be any

good when I ask her to play catch with me?"

"You were going to ask me to play catch?" Patti asked.

Mark nodded.

Patti stood and moved toward Mark, wagging her finger. "You think I'm going out and throwing a ball with you, Mark Prescott? After all that's happened? After you almost accused me of slashing Joe's tire? After you nearly got me in trouble for punching Joe? Is that what you think? Huh?"

"Well," Mark said sheepishly as he looked from Patti to Whit and then back to Patti again. "Yeah."

Patti smiled. "Okay. Let me go home and change first."

She laughed and Whit did, too, long and heartily.

Maybe things will get back to normal again, Mark thought.

Other books by Paul McCusker

Youth Ministry Comedy & Drama: Better Than Bathrobes but Not Quite Broadway
(co-author Chuck Bolte; Group Books)

Plays

Snapshots & Portraits
(Lillenas Publishing Co.)
Camp W
(Contemporary Drama Service)
Family Outings
(Lillenas Publishing Co.)
The Revised Standard Version of Jack Hill
(Baker's Play Publishing Co.)
Catacombs
(Lillenas Publishing Co.)
The Case of the Frozen Saints
(Baker's Play Publishing Co.)
The Waiting Room
(Baker's Play Publishing Co.)
A Family Christmas
(Contemporary Drama Service)
The First Church of Pete's Garage
(Baker's Play Publishing Co.)
Home for Christmas
(Baker's Play Publishing Co.)

Sketch Collections

Void Where Prohibited
(Baker's Play Publishing Co.)
Some Assembly Required
(Contemporary Drama Service)
Quick Skits & Discussion Starters
(co-author Chuck Bolte; Group Books)
Vantage Points
(Lillenas Publishing Co.)
Batteries Not Included
(Baker's Play Publishing Co.)
Souvenirs
(Baker's Play Publishing Co.)
Sketches of Harvest
(Baker's Play Publishing Co.)

Musicals

The Meaning of Life & Other Vanities
(co-author Tim Albritton; Baker's Play Publishing Co.)